BARBARA NICKEL

A Boy Asked the Wind

Illustrated by

GILLIAN NEWLAND

Red Deer Press

Published in Canada by Red Deer Press, 195 Allstate Parkway, Markham, Ontario L3R 4T8

Published in the United States by Red Deer Press, 311 Washington Street, Brighton, Massachusetts 02135

All inquiries should be addressed to Red Deer Press, 195 Allstate Parkway, Markham, Ontario L3R 4T8.

www.reddeerpress.com

10 9 8 7 6 5 4 3 2 1

Red Deer Press acknowledges with thanks the Canada Council for the Arts, and the Ontario Arts Council for their support of our publishing program. We acknowledge the financial support of the Government of Canada through the Canada Book Fund (CBF) for our publishing activities.

Canada Council for the Arts Conseil des arts du Canada

We acknowledge the financial support of the Government of Canada.
Nous reconnaissons l'appui financier du gouvernement du Canada.

Library and Archives Canada Cataloguing in Publication
Nickel, Barbara Kathleen, 1966-, author
A boy asked the wind / Barbara Nickel ; illustrator, Gillian Newland.
ISBN 978-0-88995-480-9 (paperback)
I. Newland, Gillian, author II. Title.
PS8577.I3B69 2015 jC813'.54 C2015-904308-5

Publisher Cataloging-in-Publication Data (U.S)
Nickel, Barbara, 1966-
A boy asked the wind / Barbara Nickel ; Gillian Newland.
[40] pages : color illustrations ; cm.
Summary: "A Boy Asked the Wind is a whimsical dance around the world on the shoulders of the world's most celebrated winds, starting with the Chinooks. The vivid poetry takes a young boy (and the reader) on an evocative journey from the prairies to South America to Cape Town to the Middle East and then home again. At each stop the distinctive flavor of each region's wind blows through".
ISBN: 978-0-88995-480-9 (pbk.)
1. Weather – Juvenile fiction. 2. Winds – Juvenile fiction. 3. Travel – Juvenile fiction. I.Newland, Gillian. II.Title.
[E] dc23 PZ7.N535B69 2015

Edited for the Press by Peter Carver
Cover and interior design by Kong Njo
Printed in China by Sheck Wah Tong Printing Press Ltd.

For Nicholas, who asked.

– B. N.

For B, who means the world to me.

– G. N.

A boy asked the wind, "Where do you live?"
And the wind up high in the flag shivered,
the wind down low in the grass rivered
over his toes to scatter the leaves.

The boy called again, "Where is your home?"
The wind up high in the maple hummed
the leaves free and scarlet, then hammered
down to blast against the boy's ear, "Come—

come west with me, come jag and jig
down mountainsides, over the crags
where I'm Chinook." The boy felt a tug
and a gust and a shake and a warm singing,

a warm breath around his head,
and saw a prairie huge and spread
below with snow and bison herds.
"Snow Eater's here," the boy heard,

plunging with a mighty whoosh,
horns and hooves, a mighty swish
through dry grass and coulees, rushing
everywhere until the winter vanished.

Then he and Chinook lingered to whistle
spring into the land, tussled
through shoots of silverweed, flew faster
than homecoming geese, ran past

a herd of bison pounding, leaping
over the cliff.

Nightfall. Wind and boy looped
smoke up from the fires, slipped
meat-roasting aromas under the flaps

of tipis all around. "Now I know!"
exclaimed the boy in the firelight's glow.
"This land of the Blackfoot and buffalo
is where you live!" The wind seesawed

but didn't answer. He was blowing the foam
upon an ocean way down south, roaming
far out to sea, screaming,

"Papagayo! Papagayo's come
to churn this water, mix the shallow
warm with deeper cold." So the boy followed
the warm downswirling, cold upflowing,
seething, rolling, swelling, howling

paths Papagayo stirred,
where algae bloomed like tiny stars
from feasting on cold water's stores
of healthy food.

The boy helped to stir
up one-eyed copepods, teardrop-
shaped and miniscule, who gulped
the algae feast and were gulped
by something bigger, who was eaten

by something bigger. Swish, swash—
fish ate fish ate fish ate fish
ate fish ate fish ate fish ate fish…
until a huge marlin came whooshing

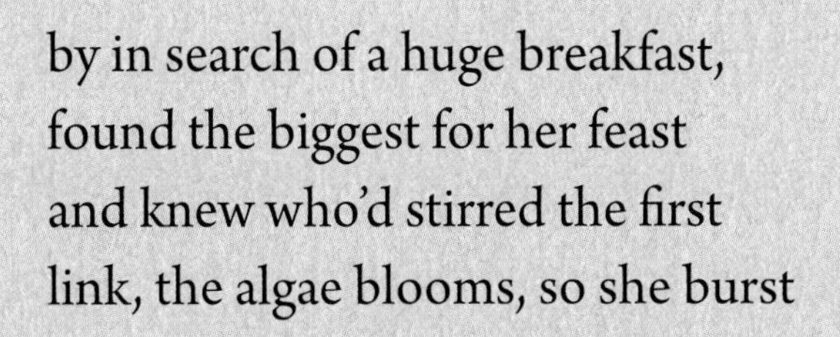

by in search of a huge breakfast,
found the biggest for her feast
and knew who'd stirred the first
link, the algae blooms, so she burst

from the water, burst right into the teeth
of the wind to offer thanks. A breath—
the boy broke surface; to the wind he gasped,
"This is your home! I know at last!"

But the wind just laughed. Then deep within the boy's ear
came the sound of travel to an ocean far:

"Doctor, Doctor, I am the Cape Doctor."
The wind's whisper grew as they swept round the corner

of the southern tip of a great continent.
"A doctor? How?" the boy asked. The wind bent
her arm round Table Mountain, sent
off pollen from its flanks where the silver trees glinted

and swayed their thanks. She moistened
the air to green the slopes, blew hello to the ghost
frogs who lived only here, blew past
dassies and porcupines, up and up fast

to the cold table top: moisture turned cloud—
the famous white tablecloth Cape Doctor laid
as she slid down the bowl to the city and said,
"Now my work begins!"

Then wildly, loudly,
Cape Doctor howled the smog away.
For fifteen nights and fifteen days
she cleared the air of fumes, of haze,
of dust and smoke from factories

and cars and trains and crazy machines!
"Is this where you live?" The wind just careened
between mountain and sea, still cleaning,
snatching hats, setting balloons free.

CHURCH
STOP

One balloon the boy watched into a speck,

speck to mountain peak,
mountain peak to army tank,
to villagers in black.

He shuddered, longed for home.
"Black for those who've died," droned
the wind Shamal. "Each summer I roam
this land between rivers, have known
its riches, and things too terrible to tell..."

And Shamal whirled a terrible whirl,
and boy and town and all were hurled
into a sandstorm orange and full
of noise.

Blinded by dust,
the boy could only hear: a blast
and clashing swords, a bomb, fist
on jaw, and spears clashing

for thousands of years, a cry
so long and deep, dark and wide,
he felt as if the world had died.
"Why?" the boy asked. "WHY?"

Shamal said, “I’m hit each time they fire
through me, the moving air.
I hurt, I hear
a boy your age crying in fear

for his soldier father gone. But can they divide
me like the land? Can they slice
me up as if I’m theirs? I ride
where I please. Do I take sides?”

Shamal sighed down to a whisper,
then rain drenched the sandstorm clear
and the boy could see stars upon stars
between his fingers, nearer than near.

Now the wind, the very one
who'd melted snow and fed the marlin,
the howling, mighty king of typhoons
who'd cleaned the air and chased balloons,

that wind became the smallest breeze,
like the breath of a baby on the boy's knees
as he stood up and saw the maple tree
of his home again. "I am Zephyr, teasing

the leaves, here and there and everywhere,
Zephyr, carrying the smallest flower,
breath of peace to a cheek when the air's
too hot, Zephyr, whispering, 'Remember…

remember…

Chinook, Papagayo, one wind,
Cape Doctor, Shamal, Zephyr, one wind
with many voices, one wind with many faces.
My home is the world.'"

ABOUT THE WIND

The wind blows all over the world in many different ways. How it blows depends on an area's climate and geographical features such as mountains or ocean or desert. Over the years the winds have been given many names. Chinook, Papagayo, Cape Doctor, Shamal, and Zephyr are a few examples. Others include the Mistral of the Mediterranean Sea, the Willy-willy cyclone of Australia, and the Haboob at the edges of the Sahara Desert in the Sudan.

CHINOOK

Also nicknamed "Snow Eater," this warm wind blows where the Prairies and the Great Plains end, and the Rocky Mountains begin. Air is warmed as it rushes down the mountains to the plains, bringing relief from the cold of winter, melting the snow; a Chinook can melt a foot of snow in a few hours. The Chinook in this story occurs at Head-Smashed-In Buffalo Jump near Fort Macleod, Alberta, where for almost 6,000 years the native people of the North American plains hunted bison by driving them off the cliffs.

ZEPHYR

Any soft, gentle breeze. Its name isn't local but ancient; Zephyros is the Greek name for the light west wind. Eight winds are carved as men into the ancient Tower of the Winds at Athens, Greece; Zephyros is shown as a youth carrying flowers into the air.

SHAMAL

This is a summer northwesterly wind blowing in the valley of the Tigris and Euphrates and the Persian Gulf in Iraq. It creates large sandstorms for many days, making a thick, blinding haze that can bring ground and air travel to a standstill.

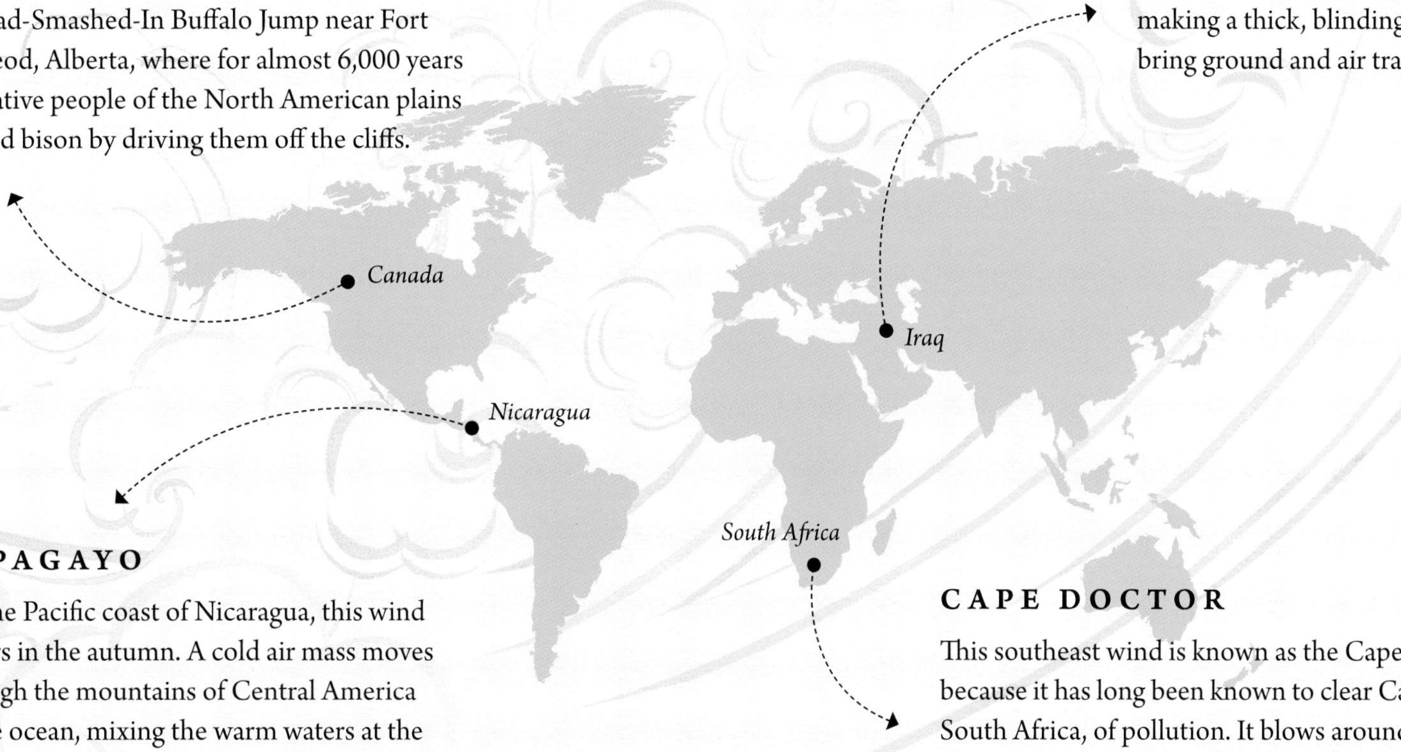

PAPAGAYO

On the Pacific coast of Nicaragua, this wind occurs in the autumn. A cold air mass moves through the mountains of Central America to the ocean, mixing the warm waters at the surface with the colder, nutrient-rich waters below. Algae grows from these nutrients, setting off an entire food chain dependent on the Papagayo wind.

CAPE DOCTOR

This southeast wind is known as the Cape Doctor because it has long been known to clear Cape Town, South Africa, of pollution. It blows around Table Mountain, bringing moisture from the ocean. When this moisture turns to cloud as the air rises, Cape Doctor lays its famous "tablecloth" of cloud upon the mountain's flat summit. Then it rushes down to Cape Town and does its "doctoring" – in November, 1936 it howled without a break for fifteen days.

GLOSSARY

copepod: A tiny animal with long antennae living in fresh or salt water, and forming an important part of the food chain.

coulee: A deep ravine with steep walls that has been formed by wind, water, or glaciers.

dassies: Resembling squirrels, dassies are sometimes called "rock rats" and can be found in rocky places in South Africa.

ghost frogs: A type of frog living in fast-moving mountain streams in South Africa.

silver trees: An evergreen tree with shiny, silver leaves that grows on the slopes of Table Mountain by Cape Town in South Africa. Silver trees are an endangered species.

silverweed: A plant with silver leaves that may grow in grassy habitats.

ACKNOWLEDGEMENTS

Special thanks to Stephanie Bolster, Peter Carver, Heinz and Lois Klassen, Jeff Marliave (Vancouver Aquarium), David Nickel, Sophia Nickel, Christopher Patton, Samir and Raya Putris, Susan Tooke, and all of my friends and family who inspired and helped with this project.

–B.N.